The Prisoner of Zenda

Anthony Hope

Retold by Sarah Courtauld

Illustrated by Simona Bursi

Reading consultant: Alison Kelly
Roehampton University

Internet Links

You can find out more about Anthony Hope
by going to the Usborne Quicklinks Website
at www.usborne-quicklinks.com and typing
in the keywords "YR Zenda".

Please note that Usborne Publishing
cannot be responsible for the content of
any website other than its own.

Series editor: Lesley Sims
Designed by Michelle Lawrence
Series designer: Russell Punter

First published in 2009 by Usborne Publishing Ltd., Usborne House,
83-85 Saffron Hill, London EC1N 8RT, England. www.usborne.com
Copyright © 2009 Usborne Publishing Ltd.

Contents

Chapter 1

On having red hair

"When are you going to *do* something with your life, Rudolf?" said my brother's wife, Rose, while I was trying to eat breakfast. "You're old enough to get a job," she went on. "Really, you've done nothing with your life except—"

"Mess around?" I said. "What's wrong with that? I don't want a job."

My remark annoyed Rose. I stroked my dark red hair, annoying her even more.

"At least your brother's hair is black, thank goodness," she said.

"Well, I like having red hair, and I like being a Ruritanian," I said. Rose scowled.

At this point, perhaps I should explain a few things.

Whenever I read books, I always skip the boring explanations, but I realize that I must explain why Rose hated my red hair so much, and why I sat in a drawing room in London and talked about being a Ruritanian. It starts with an old family scandal...

More than two hundred years ago, a handsome prince visited the English court. He had dark red hair, and an unusually long, straight nose.

The Prince fell in love with a beautiful lady and duelled with her husband to win her. Both men were wounded in the duel.

The Prince went home to Ruritania, where he later became King Rudolf I, and the lady's husband died of his wounds.

Some months later, his widow gave birth to a baby with blue eyes, an unusually long, straight nose, and dark red hair.

In every generation in that family — that is to say, in *my* family — there is one child with red hair, and one with a long straight nose. And I just happened to have both.

"Rudolf, please listen," said Rose. "You really *must* find a job. I know of one that starts in September," she added, and looked at me so sweetly I gave in.

"Fine," I said, "I'll do it." I had given her my promise, and I would stick to it. But I had six months of freedom left. I would use the time to travel to Ruritania and discover the land of my red-haired ancestors.

Chapter 2

A merry evening

When I arrived in Ruritania, the place was in a state of great excitement. A new King was to be crowned the next day. I decided to go to the capital, Streslau, to watch and stopped off in the sleepy town of Zenda on my way.

It was a bright, sunny morning, and I went for a stroll through the forest. After walking an hour or two, I sat against a tree and drifted to sleep. I was in the middle of a pleasant dream, when a rough, loud voice woke me up.

"By the devil! Shave his beard and he'd be the King!"

I opened my eyes. Two men stood over me. One was short and stout, with a bristly moustache and pale blue eyes. The other was much younger, with dark hair and a graceful, handsome face.

I scrambled to my feet.

"He's just the right height too!" muttered the older man, staring at me. He reached forwards to shake my hand. "I'm Colonel Sapt, and this is Fritz," he said. "We're servants of the King of Ruritania. May I ask… who are you?"

"Rudolf Rassendyll from England," I said.

"Rassendyll, Rassendyll," muttered Colonel Sapt. His face lit up. "By Heaven! Fritz, you know the old story, don't you?"

At that moment, a voice called out from the woods behind us. "Fritz? Fritz, where are you?"

Fritz started. "It's the King!" he said, as a young man jumped out from behind a tree. When I saw him, I gasped. Seeing me, he turned pale.

For a moment we both stood still. Apart from my beard, and a couple of inches in height, the King and I could have been twins. We gazed at each other in astonishment. Then I bowed respectfully.

"Who is this gentleman?" the bewildered King asked Colonel Sapt. Sapt whispered in the King's ear. The King frowned, then started to smile. Finally, he burst out laughing. "Cousin!" he said, slapping me on the back. "You must forgive me for being so startled. Where are you headed?"

"To the coronation," I said.

The King laughed again. "I can't wait to see my brother's face when he sees the pair of us. Well, you shall stay with us at the hunting lodge tonight."

And so, that evening I dined with Rudolf, the King of Ruritania. We ate heartily, drank much and talked merrily.

"Let us have a toast," said the King, "to our red Ruritanian hair!"

When dinner was over, Josef, the King's servant, set a dusty old flagon on the table.

"His Royal Highness, Michael, Duke of Streslau, sends you this wine with his love."

"Well, well," said the King grimly. "Does my brother think I'll be too scared to drink?

Open it up! Friends," he continued, "you may have anything I own. But don't ask me for a single drop of the wine in this bottle. I'll drink it all, to the health of that sly knave, my brother Black Michael."

With that, he gulped the wine down to the last drop. He laid his head on his arms, and that is all I can remember of the evening.

Chapter 3

A dilemma

The next morning I awoke with a start and a shiver. I was soaking wet, and Sapt was standing in front of me, holding an empty bucket. I jumped up.

"What are you doing?" I shouted.

"Nothing else would wake you," said Sapt. "Look."

In front of me the King lay stretched out on the floor. His face was as red as his hair, and he was snoring loudly. Sapt gave him a hard kick, but it made no difference.

"We've been trying to wake him for an hour," said Fritz.

I felt for the King's pulse. It was very slow. "Do you think that last bottle was drugged?" I asked.

"Yes, and by his brother, Black Michael," said Sapt, through gritted teeth.

Sapt knelt beside the King and put a hand on his back more gently. "Everyone knows Black Michael wants the throne," he went on, "and he'd give his soul to marry Princess Flavia, who's to be Queen."

"He'll never make it to the coronation. And if he isn't crowned today, he'll never be crowned," Fritz added.

"Why not?" I asked.

"The whole army will be at the coronation, with Black Michael at its head," said Sapt. "If King Rudolf isn't crowned today, Michael will be King before tomorrow."

For a moment we were all silent. Then Sapt took his pipe from his mouth and turned to me.

"As a man grows old he believes in Fate," he said. "Fate brought you here. Fate now sends you to Streslau to be crowned."

"Impossible," I muttered. "Everyone would know it was me!"

"If you shave your beard, you'd never be discovered," said Sapt. "I think you're scared."

"The King can rest here today," said Fritz. "By tomorrow he'll have recovered. He can return to the palace, and you can continue with your travels."

"But —"

"Of course, we'll die if we're found out," said Sapt. "But I'd rather die than let that knave, Black Michael, steal the throne. And he will, if you don't help."

The clock ticked fifty or sixty times. Then my face must have changed, because Sapt looked relieved. "So, you'll go?"

I nodded. I didn't seem to have a choice.

Chapter 4

The Coronation

"Long live King Rudolf!" came a shout. Every house was hung with flags, and the streets were packed with cheering crowds. Ladies stood on balconies, scattering roses before my horse. I was at the head of a grand procession, and perhaps I should have been terrified, but I was giddy with excitement. For a moment, I almost thought I really was the King.

"He's taller than I thought," I heard someone say.

"And more handsome," said another voice. (It was all just flattery, I'm sure.)

Soon the great oak doors of Streslau cathedral stood before me. For the first time, I realized the sheer madness of what I was doing. Everything was in a mist as I walked up the aisle. Only two faces stood out distinctly: the face of a pale and beautiful girl, who was gazing at me, and the face of a man with red cheeks, black hair, and dark, deep eyes.

When he saw me his jaw dropped and the helmet in his hands fell to the floor with a crash. He stared at me with hatred in his eyes.

"So that's Black Michael," I thought.

I knelt to receive the crown, and moments later, I stepped outside with the beautiful girl by my side. The crowds broke into wild applause.

"Her Royal Highness the Princess Flavia!" shouted a herald.

"When's the wedding?" someone yelled, as we stepped up into a carriage. As it rattled off down the street, the Princess turned to me.

"You know Rudolf, you look quite different today."

"Really?" I said. Her remark wasn't that surprising. But it was alarming.

"You look more thoughtful, and I'm sure you're thinner," she went on. "You look almost like a different person. Surely you haven't begun to take anything seriously?"

"Would that make you happy?" I asked, desperately trying to think of a way to change the subject.

"You know my views," she replied.

"Indeed."

It would have been handy if I did know her views. I wished I knew a single thing about her, and I secretly cursed myself for not asking Sapt what on earth I should say to her.

"Well, go on, silly," said Flavia.

"Um, what was that?"

"Go on, wave!" Flavia said. "Or have you quite forgotten how to be a king?"

As I waved to the crowds, the Princess turned to me. I realized I had never seen anyone so beautiful. She whispered into my ear: "Be careful of Michael! You must keep watch on him. He wants —"

"He wants the throne that I have," I said, "and the Princess I hope to win."

Flavia blushed, and I thought I was playing the King's part very well.

Guns fired and trumpets blared. We had arrived at the palace. That night, as I sat at the head of a state banquet, I wondered what the real King was doing.

Chapter 5

In the cellar

As darkness fell, Fritz, Sapt and I slipped out of the palace, and rode to Zenda to get the King and bring him back to Streslau.

But when we arrived at the hunting lodge, no one came to greet us. Inside, all was quiet. As Sapt walked along a corridor, he swore loudly. From under the cellar door, a red stain had spread over the floor and dried there.

Sapt sank against the wall. I tried the door. It was locked.

"Where's the King?" I said. I took my pistol, fired at the lock and the door swung open. Holding a candle above my head, I walked inside. I could see several bottles of wine, spiders crawling all over the walls, and, in the middle of the room, the body of a man lying flat on his back, with a red slit across his throat.

I knelt down and saw that it was the King's servant, Josef. I heard a shout and turned to see Sapt behind me, his eyes full of terror.

"The King? My God, the King!" he cried.

The candle's light stretched to every corner of the cellar. "The King is not here," I said.

For ten minutes or more we sat in silence, before old Sapt stamped his foot on the floor, and was himself again. "Black Michael must have the King," he declared.

24

"We must find every soldier in Streslau," said Fritz, "and attack Black Michael as soon as we can."

"Come on! Let's go to Streslau!" I said.

But old Sapt pulled out his pipe and lit it carefully, and a smile appeared on his wrinkled face. "That's right, lad," he said, "We'll go back to Streslau. The King shall be in the capital again tomorrow. The *crowned* King."

"You're crazy!" I said.

"We have to go," said Sapt. "If we return and tell people the trick we played, what do you think they'll do?"

"But Black Michael knows I'm a fake!"

"Of course," replied Sapt. "But he can hardly say, 'This isn't the King, because I've kidnapped him,' can he?"

"If you pretend to be the King, you may still save him," said Fritz.

It was a wild plan, but I knew I had been offered a chance I would never have again. "Sapt," I said, "I'll do it."

Chapter 6

An adventure with a tea table

Aking may have a hard life, but a man
pretending to be a king has a harder
one. The next day, Sapt told me my duties,
my likes and dislikes. He told me that
the King liked white wine and dogs, and
hated cats and too much salt. There were
a thousand rules to remember, and I soon
forgot them all.

The only reason I wasn't caught was
that no one imagined that anyone could
do something so dangerous and stupid as
impersonate a King. No one except Black
Michael, who paid me a visit that very day.

"Your Majesty," he said, with a smile on his lips and a murderous look in his eyes.

"Dear brother," I said, "how kind of you to send me that bottle of wine. It gave me so much energy for the coronation."

"I'm glad," said Michael. "Your good health is always my first concern."

"How lucky I am to have such a loyal brother," I observed.

"I have a friend who would like to meet you," Michael said. "A loyal servant of the King: Rupert Hentzau."

A handsome young man strolled into the room, and gave me an insolent smile.

"He's in on the secret too," I thought. When I was finally rid of them both, I turned to Sapt. "Who was that?"

"Rupert Hentzau is Black Michael's bravest soldier, and the best sword fighter in the country," he replied. "He has two hobbies. The first is falling in love with beautiful women..."

"And the other?" I asked.

"Defeating his enemies. He'll be happy to cut your throat just as soon as he gets the chance."

So now I had not one deadly enemy, but two.

The next evening, Sapt walked into my dressing room and threw a letter on the table.

To the King,
At the end of New Avenue, there is a
house with a large garden. In the garden is
a summer house. Wait there at midnight,
and you will find a faithful friend who
can tell you news of great importance.
Antoinette

"Who's Antoinette?" I asked him.

"Black Michael's sweetheart," Sapt replied. "If Michael becomes King, he'll marry Princess Flavia. Antoinette will do anything to stop him from taking the throne – so she can keep Black Michael for herself. But make no mistake," he went on, "this letter is a trap. If you go, you'll never get out of the garden alive."

"Perhaps it is a trap. But I believe that woman, and I will go," I told him.

"It'll be the death of you," said Sapt.

"I'll go, or go back to England," I said.

"So be it," said Sapt with a sigh.

And thus, at midnight, Sapt and I arrived at the house.

"I'll wait here," he said. "If I hear a shot —"

"Run away," I said. "There's no point in us both being killed."

Sapt waited with the horses, while I crept into the garden, my revolver at the ready. A large building loomed in front of me, and I pushed open the door.

"Shut the door," came a whisper. A beautiful woman stood in the darkness. "I know what you are doing, Mr. Rassendyll," she hissed. "In twenty minutes three men will be here to kill you. You must be gone by then. Michael plans to kill you, murder the King and marry Princess Flavia."

"Where's the King now?" I asked.

"In his castle at Zenda. When you cross the drawbridge, you come to- What's that?"

There were footsteps outside.

"They're here too soon," she hissed.

"Rassendyll," came a voice. It was Rupert Hentzau. "Let us in. We have an offer for you. We won't shoot."

I peered through a chink in the door.
Three revolvers pointed at it.

"What's your offer?" I asked.

"We'll take you safely to the frontier,
and give you fifty thousand pounds, if you
promise never to return."

"I accept," I said. "Let me out, and I
promise not to fire before you do."

In the bare summer house was a small,
iron tea table. I picked it up. When I
turned it on its side, it made a fine shield
for my head and body.

"Stand back," I ordered Antoinette
quietly. "Gentlemen," I said more loudly, "if
you would open the door?"

I smiled as the door swung open. With a shout, I charged through. Three shots rang out and battered my shield. The table crashed into the three men, and they and I and the brave tea table all tumbled down the steps of the summerhouse.

"Ha!" I jumped to my feet as a shot whizzed past my ear. Black Michael and Rupert Hentzau lay in a tangle under the tea table, and another soldier lay sprawled on his back.

Rupert raised his revolver and fired again. I fired back, and raced away like a hare. I tore back to where Sapt was still waiting and clapped him on the back. "Let's go home, old man," I said with a laugh.

"You're safe!" he cried. "And what on earth is so funny?"

"I beat them with a tea table!" I said, jumping up on to my horse.

As we rode away, I felt particularly proud because I'd kept my promise, and not fired before they did.

Chapter 7

A grand ball

"We must go straight to Zenda," I said to Sapt the next morning.

"The preparations are all made," said Sapt. "But there's one more thing you must do as King. I've arranged for you to give a ball for Princess Flavia tonight. You must ask her to marry you. The people desire it."

"I won't!" I said. "I refuse to make a fool of her. How could I trick her? What happens when the real King returns?"

Sapt said nothing. But he knew I would obey him, despite my protests, for I had fallen in love with the Princess.

That night, as I danced a waltz with Flavia, curious eyes and eager whispers surrounded us.

Afterwards, we wandered together into a little room. Stammering, I told her I loved her. Her reply took me by surprise.

"How is it that I love you now, Rudolf? I... I never did before you were crowned."

I was filled with happiness. She loved me – not the King!

"Why are you so happy to hear that I didn't love you before?" she said, laughing.

"If I were not the King," I said, "if I were only a private gentleman..."

Flavia put her hand in mine. "If you were a convict in Streslau prison, I'd still love you," she said, her eyes shining with happiness.

"Flavia," I blurted out, "I am not the K—"

"Beg your pardon, sir," said a gruff voice. Sapt's face appeared at the window. "The cardinal wishes to say goodnight to you."

I caught the angry look in his eyes. I do not know how long he had been standing there, but he had come just in time.

Chapter 8

A desperate plan

The next morning I set out for Zenda, with Sapt, Fritz, and ten strong men. We stayed in a fine house in the woods, close to Black Michael's castle.

Sapt went out riding and came back with a triumphant look in his eyes. He'd paid a servant – Johann – to tell him where the King was. "At the end of the bridge in the castle gatehouse, there are two rooms cut into the stone," he said. "The outer room has two guards. The King is held in chains in the inner room."

"Does the King's room have a window?" I asked.

"The window is filled with a pipe, just big enough to fit a body into," Sapt answered.

"If an attacker reaches the outer room, one guard will fight him off. The other will murder the King and send his body down the pipe. The pipe leads into the moat. The King's body will never be found."

Sapt turned pale. "The King is very sick," he added. "A doctor is being held prisoner with him in his cell. He can barely walk, or speak. I'm afraid he may not live long..."

For a while, we sat in bewildered silence.

"It's a hard nut to crack," Sapt finished. "But we must attack tonight."

"I think I have an idea," I replied. "Is Antoinette in the castle?"

"She is," said Sapt.

"Then I hope she'll help us. Our lives may depend on it." I scribbled a note to Antoinette and gave it to Johann.

Antoinette ~
At midnight, call out for Black Michael.
Say that Rupert Hentzau is attacking you.
It's our only chance to save the King.
Rudolf

If all went to plan, Johann would let Sapt into the castle after nightfall. Then, when Antoinette called for help, Black Michael would come running and fall into the murderous arms of Sapt. Meanwhile, I would try to rescue the King.

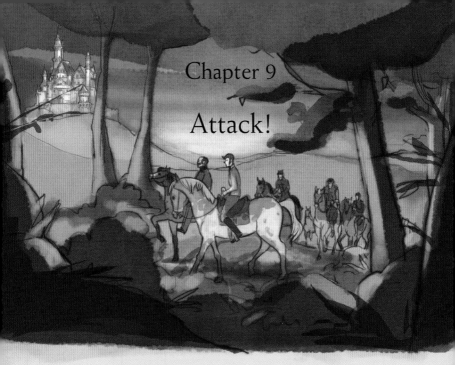

Chapter 9

Attack!

In darkness, our party set out for the castle. Sapt and I rode first, with ten soldiers following us. We clung to shadows, and rode as quietly as we could. When we arrived Sapt knocked very lightly on the door. The servant, Johann opened it, and Sapt and the others slipped inside.

I decided to stay outside and keep watch. Crouching down by the gatehouse, I prepared for a long wait.

The clock struck twelve, then one, then a light shone through a window.

"Help! Michael, help!" came a cry, followed by a shriek of pure terror.

I was tingling in every nerve.

"What's the matter?" roared Black Michael. "I'm coming up!"

"Help, Michael, it's Rupert Hentzau!" screamed Antoinette.

Sapt should be striking Black Michael now, I thought. But a moment later, I saw Black Michael still upright in Antoinette's bedroom. My heart sank. What had happened to Sapt?

I heard Black Michael shout, "What's going on? Where is he?" There were running footsteps and then Black Michael shouted again. "Rupert, you sly dog! How could you attack Antoinette?"

Then Rupert's voice: "I did no such thing!"

"Ha! Do you expect me to believe that?"

I heard the clash of crossed swords as the two men began to fight.

"Come on Michael," said Rupert and Black Michael cried out.

The next thing I knew, Rupert had jumped onto a windowsill, laughing and waving his sword in his hand.

Blood was pouring down his face. He laughed again as he flung himself headlong into the moat.

As Rupert jumped, a guard peered out of the door beside me.

"What's going on?" he said. I struck him with all the strength I had. He fell without a word, and I knelt beside him.

"The keys! The keys!" I muttered, rifling through his pockets. At last I had them. Seizing the largest key, I tried it in the lock of the door that led to the King's prison, and found myself at the top of a flight of stone steps.

I took a lantern from the wall, and stood still for a moment, listening.

"Who the devil can that be?" I heard a voice say. It came from behind the door at the bottom of the stairs.

Another voice hissed: "Shall we kill him?"

I strained to hear the answer, and I could have cried with relief when it came.

"Wait a bit. There'll be trouble if we strike too soon."

There was a moment's silence. I heard the bolt of the door being drawn back and put out the lantern at once.

"It's dark, do you have a light?" said
a voice.

I rushed down the stairs and flung
myself through the door, sword in hand.

Two guards stood before me. One staggered backwards while the other drew his sword.

"Ha!" I cried, and rushed madly at one of the guards. I drove him against the wall.

He fought bravely, but he was no great swordsman, and in a moment he lay on the floor before me.

I spun around, but the other guard was gone. He had rushed into the King's room, slammed the door behind him, and even now was at work, inside. And he would have killed the King, and perhaps me too, had it not been for one brave man.

When I forced the door open, the King was standing in the corner of the room. I barely recognized him. His chained hands were at his sides, and he was laughing like a lunatic. The guard and the King's doctor were struggling in the middle of the room.

The doctor had no weapon to defend himself and all too soon he was backed up against the wall with nowhere to go.

With a cry of triumph,
the guard drove his sword through the
poor doctor, and turned to me.

We fought sword to sword: silently,
sternly, and hard. He knew more tricks than
I did and a smile flickered across his face as
his sword cut deep into my arm.

I know he would have killed me, for he was the best swordsman I had ever fought, but as he pressed me to the wall, the lunatic of a King in the corner jumped up, shouting:

"It's cousin Rudolf! I'll help you, cousin Rudolf!" Picking up a chair, he staggered over to us.

"Come on, Sire!" I encouraged him. "Come and share the fun! Strike his legs!"

With an oath, the guard turned round to face the King. He made a fierce swipe at him, and the King fell to the floor with a cry. The guard turned back to me, but he stepped in a pool of blood on the floor. For a second he slipped, and I was on him.

I drew my sword across his throat, and he fell against the body of the doctor.

Was the King dead? I rushed to his side. It seemed as if he were: there was a great cut across his forehead.

I knelt to hear if he was breathing, but as I did, I heard footsteps outside. In another second, I could be surrounded by Black Michael's men.

I took my sword and dragged myself up the stairs. Where was Sapt? Had our men taken the castle? I stood for a second, catching my breath as I tore a strip off my shirt and wrapped it around my aching, bleeding arm.

At that moment, I would have given anything to see Sapt appear.

And then I heard a laugh. It was a merry, scornful laugh – the laugh of Rupert Hentzau. Sapt and his men couldn't have taken the castle. If they had, Rupert would be dead. I ran to a window and looked out.

In the middle of the bridge stood Rupert, sword in hand. His white shirt was spattered with blood. "Michael! You dog!" he shouted. "Come out and fight me. Come out, if you wish to win Antoinette."

I watched spellbound, waiting to see what would happen.

Then Sapt's voice roared from inside the castle. "Black Michael is dead!" Seconds later, Sapt himself strode onto the bridge.

Sapt walked towards Rupert, a group of his men behind him. Slowly and deliberately, he raised his revolver and took careful aim.

Rupert was trapped. He would have to rush forward to overcome Sapt and if he turned, Sapt would shoot as he ran away.

"Goodbye," Rupert said. And before Sapt had a chance to fire, Rupert bowed gracefully, and dived off the bridge into the moat once more.

I had to move quickly. To have any chance of catching him, I'd have to dive in too.

I leaped into the water and swam until my lungs were bursting. Meanwhile, Rupert had crossed the moat and climbed the wall on the other side.

"Rudolf Rassendyll, the little actor," he said, pointing his sword at my heart. If I had tried to climb up, he would have sliced me in two. "Aren't you getting cold?"

"Not at all," I replied. "It's a lovely night for a swim."

Rupert disappeared from view. When I reached the top of the wall, he was fleeing into the forest.

I chased Rupert for what seemed like hours. When I finally caught up with him, he was leaping onto a horse.

"So, is the King dead?" he asked scornfully.

"I don't know," I said.

"You fool," he sneered, and I lunged at him with my sword.

He had the advantage of height but I managed to cut his cheek. He struck back and I rushed at him again. One or both of us would have died, but at that moment, there came a shout from behind us.

"Rudolf!" It was Fritz, my faithful friend, with a revolver in his hand.

Rupert smiled. "Goodbye, Rudolf Rassendyll," he said. He struck his horse hard with his heels, and raced away.

"Ride after him, Fritz!" I gasped.

Instead, Fritz jumped from his horse and ran to me. The blood from my wound was staining the ground.

"If you won't chase him, give me your horse, and I will," I said. I staggered to my feet, got as far as the horse, and collapsed beside it. "Is the King dead?" I gasped.

"He's alive," said Fritz, "Thanks to you."

I tried to speak, but found I could not. My eyes closed and I heard no more.

Chapter 10

Past, present, future?

And so our grand scheme was almost complete. The King was taken to a room inside the castle, where he lay recovering. We might have swapped places without anyone knowing, had it not been for Princess Flavia.

When she heard the King was hurt, she rode straight to Zenda. I knew I could never see her again. But she saw me walking through the forest with Sapt, and galloped up to us.

"Are you hurt, my love?" she called and jumped off her horse. I cast my eyes to the ground. Before I could say or do anything, she kissed me.

"Do not kiss him, your Highness," whispered Sapt. "He is not the King."

"What kind of strange joke is this?" said

Flavia, laughing. "Are you telling me I don't know my own love? Rudolf!"

"He is not the King, your Highness," Sapt said again. This time, from his grave face, she knew he was not joking.

"The King is in the castle," said Sapt. "This gentleman..."

"Look at me Rudolf!" Flavia cried. "Tell me what this means!"

I raised my eyes to look at her. "Forgive me," I said. "I am not the King."

She fell, weeping, into my arms.

That evening, Sapt told her everything. Before I left, I begged Flavia to come with me. But she refused, saying sadly, "My duty is with my country and my King." And so I said goodbye to her, and to Zenda, for the last time.

Sapt and I rode through a night and a day, until we came to a train station just beyond the border of Ruritania. A plume of smoke was rising from a train in the distance.

"We've done well between us," I said.

"Well lad, you would have made the finest King of them all," said Sapt. "But Fate doesn't always make the right men kings."

As the train drew into the station, we embraced. I climbed aboard and was gone.

Once again, I was Rudolf Rassendyll, an Englishman with little wealth and no power.

"You've done nothing but mess around all summer," said my brother, and my sister-in-law Rose joined in.

"What a lazy boy you are. Now, about this job – it's at an embassy, in Ruritania, in Streslau."

"I won't take it," I said, immediately.

"Oh Rudolf," she sighed, "Will you never get a job?"

But I did get a job, and settled down. Now I live a quiet, simple sort of life in England.

Sometimes I wonder if I will ever again have the chance to mix in great affairs, to match my wits against my enemies, and fight a good fight. But whether my dream will come true, or is just a fancy I cannot tell.

About Anthony Hope

Anthony Hope was born in London in 1863. He grew up to be a lawyer, and thought up the idea of *The Prisoner of Zenda* while walking around London. It only took him a month to write.

When it was published, the novel was so successful that he decided to give up his job to be a full-time writer.

He also wrote a sequel, called *Rupert of Hentzau*, and several other books set in imaginary countries. In all, he wrote more than 30 books and plays. Anthony Hope died at the age of 70, in 1933.